TITLE

THE SPIRIT SWORN

Chapter One

Lightning streaked upward enlightening a hooded figure remaining external the fundamental medical clinic building, unminding of the heavy storm prepared to drench even the most intrepid deep down. Looking vertical the figure fixed their eye on the expected objective, a room on the farthest corner, twelfth floor.

Don't worry about it.

They had been climbing coconut trees since they were three years of age, some far taller than the undertaking laid before them. With a break of knuckle and neck, the figure jumped to the side of the structure, moving consistently starting with one gallery then onto the next sometimes scaling an uncovered drainpipe until they arrived at their objective.

Landing daintily on the overhang, the figure lurked up to the glass entryway, looking in. The room was deserted, save for the solitary occupant in the bed. The entryway slid open without opposition and back shut similarly as quietly. Pushing the hood back the figure got a brief look at their appearance in the entryway enlightened by a cut of lightning.

A young lady, mid twenties with cocoa skin and a somewhat innocent hair style gazed back. The main thing damaging her excellence was a long scar stumbling into the right half of her face and another simply over the scaffold of her nose. The scars ran profound as the more extended of the two prompted a cowhide eye fix masking further harm. She immediately abandoned the entryway and ventured to the bed, shattered at what she found.

Prior to her lay a lady of a similar age, so comparative in appearance it was all the while unsettling after so much time. The lady's eyes were shut as she took battered inhales behind a breathing device. Her regularly brilliant skin held a debilitated paleness. The young lady in the shroud pushed ahead barely enough to brush the long, wavy hair away from the other's brow and spot a delicate kiss upon it.

Coming to down, she took the young lady's hand in her own while looking at her wounds. The young lady in the bed had the whole left half of her middle vigorously swathed. A few red messes specking the delicate texture showed where the projectiles had entered, and at times, left. Three shots. She had heard them. Watched with dismay as the other young lady fell; wished to rush to her guide yet couldn't.

"It's me, Mari." She murmured into the other's ear. "It's Tina. I'm here and all will be great. You will be alright."

Tina sat back standing by rigidly for a reaction, any sign that Mari was not so lost as she appeared. Seconds ticked by and she could hear strides in the lobby. She prepared herself to make a speedy retreat yet the means moved past the entryway and down the passage. She hadn't actually expected organization, it was 1:30 toward the beginning of the day, and the medical clinic was everything except deserted at this hour. Right external the entryway, she could see the resting monitor, bombing horrendously at his specific employment. A sound from the bed pulled her consideration. Mari aired out her eyes and gazed in dismay.

"Tina?" she murmured dryly, even as her vision was obstructed by the other young lady inclining forward to kiss her face tenderly. "How?"

"I snuck in, we don't have a lot of time. I needed to realize you were alright."

"You ... shouldn't be... here... " Mari panted, torment gnawing at each syllable. Tina couldn't be here, she would get them both killed. They were foes! How is it that she could disregard that?

"I know! I just needed to see you. You get that, don't you?" Tina was grasping her hand furiously with tears gushing from her unharmed eye. "I pardon you! That is the reason you need to get through. So we can fix this! Together."

Mari shut her eyes, breathing weighty behind the cover since this was really much for her. Tina pardoned her? She couldn't and shouldn't. Mari was a beast; she had dealt with that. How is it that anyone could pardon her for what she had done, particularly to her close family? She could feel her cognizance getting away when Tina drove something into her palm and shut her fingers firmly around it.

"So you'll forever recall that you're adored." Tina murmured against her temple prior to kissing her again and delivering her hand.

"No... Tina... " She called weakly to her.

"I'll be back soon. I guarantee." She heard not long before her eyes slid shut, banishing her back into dimness.

"The harm was broad. One more inch to one side and she would have been killed immediately. It will require a little while for her to recuperate, in the event that not months."

"Indeed, even with the ... 'improvements'?"

"The 'improvements' are the main explanation she has endure this far."

Mari moved marginally in bed. There were individuals talking, two individuals, about her it appeared. Her psyche was obfuscated as she attempted to recall. She had been on a phase, in full dress uniform. Could it be said that she was giving a discourse? At the point when a man emerged from the group... he had a firearm!

She was shot!

Multiple times. Then, at that point, such an uproar and disarray and... Bettina! Tina had been here; she had come final evening. Was that a fantasy? Mari fixed her clench hand and the hard article delving into her palm affirmed it.

"Tina... " She groaned before she understood. The others in the room immediately mixed to her side.

"She's awakening! Skipper? Would you be able to open your eyes?" One of the voices provoked her. Mari gulped hard and attempted to agree. Gradually her eyes separated, giving a cruel line of light access. She murmured at the attack on her faculties and the room immediately obscured. "Is that better? We should attempt once more."

This time when she woke up, the agony was passable and there were two concerned faces hanging over her. One was clearly a specialist deciding from the white sterile jacket and the spotlight he was waving in her face. The different was a maritime official such as herself, however she didn't remember him. She simply minded to see one individual right now.

"Where is she?" She croaked, her throat crude from the breathing cylinder that had been eliminated a couple of hours earlier. "Where's my sister?" The two men shared a confounded look before the official made some noise.

"Please accept my apologies Captain. Maybe your wounds have impacted your memory however you… you're a vagrant, no family to talk about. Certainly no sister, though it pains me to say so."

No! That was clearly false. She was genuine! She had been there only a couple of hours prior. These men were misleading her and there should be an explanation. Indeed, even in her sedated state, she understood that whatever Tina had given her could be hazardous whenever found. She faked a fit of agony to fold the item rapidly under her leg, underneath the covers. The specialist surged forward, actually looking at her breathing and changing her I.V.

She would truly not liked to rest once more, so when the specialist went to usher the official out she squeezed the line, keeping any additional medication from getting to her. She realized she was unable to keep that up for long as her whole left side was immobilized and she would begin to feel it rapidly without drugs. All she wanted was a moment to take a gander at Tina's gift.

Squirming around she hauled the item out and laid it on her stomach. The specialist had left her room and the lights were faint, so she was allowed to explore. The item being referred to was an oval memento, cut out of the best ivory. Mari followed the memento affectionately with her fingers. She knew this; it had been their moms. The engraving outwardly read "Two sovereigns, One crown", something her mom had consistently let them know growing up, advising them that they shared her heart similarly.

She squeezed delicately on the jewel close to the top and it busted open to uncover an image of two young ladies, indistinguishable in appearance sitting across their mom's lap. Mari had nearly failed to remember the amount she and Tina had appeared to be similar as youngsters; so much had changed from that point forward. Such countless wrongs.

A tear descended her face, then, at that point, another. What was the deal? For what reason would I be able to recall more? Furthermore for what reason did they need her to suppose Tina was only a dream; an invention of her creative mind? The injuries in her side started to erupt, flagging the remainder of the medications in her framework were fading however the inclination didn't be anything contrasted with the hurt in her heart. She needed to sort this out before any other individual looked into Tina. Tucking the memento back under her leg, she drew some solace from the vibe of the smooth, cool item against her skin.

Assuming she planned to observe replies, she was unable to do it from this medical clinic bed. Mari expected to improve and quick. The most effective way to do that was to rest, for the occasion, so she hesitantly delivered the I.V. line allowing herself to disappear, considering Tina and more joyful occasions.

"I'll be back soon. I guarantee."

The last thing her sister had told her. She trusted past expectation that it was valid.

Chapter two

The dissident base was a wonder of innovation, a faultless blend of old and new. Cut from the essence of a precipice, it flaunted submerged lakes and streams, any of which prompted the immense sea past. In the harbor sat an assortment of oceanic vehicles, most strikingly the leader having a place with Tina and her family.

Past the docks lay the genuine base, a progression of caverns and sinkholes changed into open to residing space including workplaces, homes, an amazing arsenal and a very much loaded clinic that matched even the most incredible in-land medical clinic.

On some random surface one could observe shining electrical boards fashioned into strong stone.

Individuals of Bridgetown and the encompassing municipalities had built an agreeable little society however it was deficient with regards to the one thing they horribly wanted... opportunity.

Barbados and all the encompassing islands had been surpassed by an especially loathsome power. The very power that had scarred Tina, almost killed Mari and obliterated their family. The resistance was driven forward on the strength of their chief and Tina would not rest until she'd had her reprisal yet for the present, there were additional squeezing matters...

The dauntless pioneer sat behind her work area gazing vacantly at the divider. She was unable to think, couldn't focus on everything except the wrecked state with which she had thought that she is darling sister. Mari was scarcely sticking to life when she had left her prior that morning and presently she held on to see whether she had been short of what was needed in going to her. A sound from the entryway pulled her consideration.

"The chief... ?" She asked likely, requiring affirmation that Marisol was all the while battling, that she would be there when Tina split away this evening to see her.

"She's as yet alive. They really anticipate that she should make a total recuperation," the courier told her with an incredulity in his voice, "yet it will not be fast."

Tina gestured mutely and excused the young fellow with an occupied wave.

She's alive! What's more she will be alright.

However, a long recuperation represented an alternate test. While it would give her more opportunity to attempt to break her sister's customizing, it additionally implied she would chance herself and the agitators each time she broke into the emergency clinic. She asked her gift had not been found; it was in a snapshot of shortcoming that she had left it in any case.

Tina would recover it this evening, since Mari realized what
was in question.

She got the outlined photograph of the two sitting around her
work area. It had been required 5 years earlier, when the
sister's were rebels battling against a bad system, cruising the
seven oceans. Before they were caught, before each supported
the horde of scars they presently showed, before they
transformed her sister into a beast. She would get Mari back.
This was the break she had been sitting tight for since that
pivotal evening. She was unable to come up short. A thump on
the door jamb interfered with her insights.

"What?" She shouted more cruelly than she needed to.

"Please accept my apologies... assuming this is an awful time...
" Tina looked up to see Lt. Troy Parker standing right inside
the entryway. He appeared to be half ready to beat a hurried
retreat, as she had been not exactly inviting all of a sudden.
Tina feigned exacerbation, reviling deep down.

"Did you really want something, lieutenant?" She put
additional accentuation on his position, reminding him not so
quietly that she was in control. He disregarded the hit and
ventured inside shutting the entryway behind him.

Troy stepped toward her work area, his long tan appendages
appeared to fill the workplace with his quality. He ran a hand
generally through his short dim hair before earthy colored
eyes secured in hers.

"I was stressed over you. I went by your quarter's the previous evening to check whether you were OK... thinking about the conditions... yet you were no more."

"I'm fine." She answered coolly however the two of them realized she was lying. "Moreover, my whereabouts are no longer your anxiety, right?"

"Let's go Tina! I know we're not... whatever we were previously, however I actually care about you. You went to see her didn't you?"

Tina overlooked his inquiry and returned to gazing at the image in her grasp. How could he come in here and carry on like he gave it a second thought? Mari almost passed on as a result of him; it had been one of his men that broke position and shot her sister without a second thought. "Didn't you?!" He requested once more.

"Indeed! Obviously, I did." She replied close to tears. "You can't tell anybody."

"Tina... " He started yet was cut off.

"Five years, Troy. That was the nearest I have been to my sister in FIVE YEARS." She didn't attempt to conceal the tears as they moved down her cheeks. "She knew me. Knew what My identity was. Every one of the occasions she's seen me since that day, there was never any acknowledgment until the previous evening."

"How can that be the case? I thought the fundamental objective of the writing computer programs was to eradicate your previous personality?"

"It is. However, imagine a scenario in which, consider the possibility that the injury caused an error or something like that. She kicked the bucket Troy. At the scene and again on the table... " She followed off in light of the fact that the picture of paramedics beating on her sister's horrendous chest caused the torture of the beyond couple of years to appear to be unimportant.

That scene played again and again to her on an unwavering circle. Mari on the stage with her standard dress uniform and the porcelain veil they made her wear to mask her face. She had looked so magnificent in her white coat, the very coat that stained with red as liquid lead tore through her middle. Tina shivered at the idea and folded her arms over herself. She's alive. She reminded herself and right now, that made a difference the most.

"What are you going to do?"

"First," she extended her jaw out and cleaned her face generally to eliminate any obvious tears. "To start with, I will go let my mom know that Mari is as yet alive. The rest... I'll sort that out later. The only thing that is important now is I at long last get an opportunity to make it right."

Five years seemed like such a limited ability to focus it had turned into a lifetime for the St. John twins. Marisol and Bettina St. John were brought into the world on the little island of Barbados to common guardians. Later the family would move to Bridgetown, the capital. Their dad August or Auggie as the island called him, was an angler, ingraining in his little girls an adoration for the untamed water. He had dim hair and blue eyes, his skin tanned from extended periods adrift. When they were large sufficient he had taken them out with him, trained them to peruse the flows, explore by the stars.

Their mom, Gaia was a doctor, who tended the family and ensured her little girls were never desirous of each other in the middle of patients. "Two sovereigns, one crown", she would berate them in her wonderful voice, touched with island lingo. Her skin was brilliant and her hair hung in huge dark twists that landed delicately on solid shoulders. The young ladies had been carbon copies of her and each other besides. The main contrast in the two was a small mole over Tina's lip. They were approaching their seventeenth birthday celebration when the tides changed.

Another power had emerged in the islands, a corporate Navy that vowed to carry request to the regressive individuals. This company loathed the basic lives individuals decided to lead, needing to take advantage of the rich regular assets that all on the island shared similarly. Their dad, Auggie, had been quick to revolt. He was considerably more than a prepared angler. Auggie was from the principle land and had served numerous years as a designer on board a British maritime vessel prior to becoming hopelessly enamored with the islands; it's kin, and above all their mom. His vessel was something other than a normal fishing boat. He'd fabricated it himself, a great 70 ft. behemoth named "The Black Hammer". It flaunted a smooth dark completion and a monumental dark banner flew from the pole bearing a shining crown held tight a mallet.

At the point when the Snow Corporation, as they called themselves, heard there was previous Navy man among its occupants, they quickly looked to enroll Auggie. Subsequent to being straight declined, Snow Corp. pushed ahead with its arrangements to carry the islands into the future they imagined regardless of whether forcibly. During one such occurrence, Snow Corp. vessels obstructed every one of the harbors, requesting that nobody could enter or leave without settling an expense.

This had rankled Auggie continually as he trusted the ocean to be free and no man reserved the privilege to prevent one more from accommodating his family. The people group was parted with regards to the best way in which to address this new test. Numerous yearned for the alleged enhancements that Snow Corp. was promising, while others, their dad included, trusted it to be a stratagem to hold onto control of the islands assets.

Auggie stood firm in his conviction and acquired a tremendous after when probably his dearest companion was gunned somewhere around Snow vessels while attempting to leave the harbor without covering the duty. Individuals had become detainees in their own homes, the neighborhood government having been sufficiently guileless enough to give Snow Corp. practically unlimited authority with expectations of filling their pockets. The head of their collaboration, Bradford Snow, had demonstrated to be a commendable and savage adversary. Impending common conflict appeared to just fuel his bid for power. Move must be made.

Auggie and a little gathering of dissidents started subverting Snow Corps' commodity ships, keeping their valuable assets from being ravaged. The Black Hammer turned into an image for the disobedience and soon Auggie himself became known as "August the Black", rebel privateer. Auggie had contacted his previous partners in the naval force however was educated that the world in general was in mayhem and the individuals who figured out how to discover a lasting sense of harmony had no goal of intruding in the issues of a little insignificant gathering of islands.

In any event, when Auggie talked about the reports encompassing Snow Corps' enrollment strategies, he was denied help. He would need to assume control over the battle. Through this he had attempted to safeguard his family from the monstrous real factors of the contention they were battling yet after almost three years, he had no real option except to bring the family locally available The Black Hammer for all time. It had become excessively hazardous for them to remain in one spot for long as Snow Corp. had put a silly abundance on Auggie's head.

Before their 20th birthday celebration, the young lady's had become an incredible privateers themselves, in any event, taking on monikers. Bettina took after their dad and started referring to herself as "Dark Betty", wearing a dull shrouded coat and a beat up dark tee with skull and crossbones. Marisol then again, regularly put herself at incredible individual danger to help individuals of the island, provoking numerous to consider her a "Holy person". The name stuck and appeared to be suitable, as it was a subsidiary of the family name. Her uniform comprised of her dad's dress uniform coat tossed over whatever she turned out to be wearing that day and a porcelain cover.

It had happened to the family from the beginning that covering the young ladies' personalities was the most effective way to guard them. Their mom, Gaia, remained generally in the background keeping an eye on displaced people and vagrants, orchestrating safe entry for these to different grounds. She loathed sending her youngsters and spouse off to battle yet additionally knew the outcomes in the event that they didn't. She implored each night for all three's protected return, a supplication that in the long run, definitely, went unanswered.

It had been a strike like some other. Board unobtrusively, incapacitate the boat, eliminate the products and free any detainees. That had been the arrangement. As usual: Auggie lead, sword drawn, with Tina behind him employing her own sharp edge and Mari covering their flank with rifle close by. Their undertakings were cultivated with rehearsed accuracy, Auggie lead his little girls onto the primary deck where they were trapped by Snow's powers!

A frantic battle with Snow's officials resulted, felling many revolutionaries. The family battled with enthusiasm, declining to be taken effectively however were at last overpowered by the sheer quantities of rivals. At the point when it was everywhere, the family had to stoop on the deck, bound and choked before their definitive adversary, Bradford Snow himself.

"About damn time we got you." He had murmured to Auggie prior to taking out a gun and firing the man in the chest!

The two young ladies shouted behind their gags, sickened by seeing their cherished dad lying dead on the deck before them. That second, in any case, had just been the start of the revulsions anticipating the two young ladies. Snow's maritime power had become inconceivably quick because of his taking young people from the islands and compelling them into administration. Nobody knew precisely the way that he had done it however the sisters viewed the strategies as more sickening than anybody envisioned.

Once eliminated from the boat, the young ladies were taken aground to Snow's principle compound for "reconditioning" which included a combination of medication treatment, torment and sometimes computerized improvements. For a really long time the young ladies were beaten, tormented and sedated with an end goal to get them to surrender their kindred revolutionaries and swear loyalty to Snow. They would not be broken and every night when they were gotten back to their cell, the two would twist into each other on one little bunk and nod off.

Their dedication would be their ruin.

Chapter Three

Tina distinctly remembered the night when *everything* had changed.

An officer had tried to assault her sister at knifepoint inside their little cell. Tina had been nearly unconscious from the day's tortures when she heard her sister screaming, dragging her out of a pain-induced haze. She opened her eyes to find Mari thrown against a wall with a knife to her throat while a young officer tried desperately to unbutton his pants with one hand. There was a thin line of blood on Mari's neck where the blade was already digging in. Her sister's eyes were wide with terror but she was too weak to fight back.

"**NO**! Leave her alone!"

She had lunged at his back with everything she had left, ripping him away from Mari. Her sister dropped painfully to the ground and the officer swung the blade wildly, off balance from her attack. The first time it met her face, Tina thought she would black out from the searing pain. The second cut was shallow and barely registered to her shocked system.

She had fallen to her knees, screaming in pain and terror, unable to defend herself. The officer kicked her savagely as she blacked out from the blood loss, Mari screaming in the background.

The next time she awoke, several hours had passed. Her face burned intensely and she found she could only open one eye. When she raised a hand to investigate, it was quickly but gently pulled away. She had followed the hand to gaze up into her sister's stricken face. Tina realized then that her head was pillowed in Mari's lap and she was lying somewhat awkwardly on the bunk in their cell. Mari had tucked her hand back under the blanket and hugged her tighter.

"I was *so scared*..." she had whispered against her sister's forehead. "I thought he had killed you and it was all my fault."

"My face..."

Tina's voice had been hoarse with pain. She knew something was wrong because their captors had never before bothered to tend their wounds after an altercation.

Mari had kissed her forehead and just kept whispering "I can't let them hurt you anymore."

Tina hadn't known what that meant until the following morning when two burly guards had come in to retrieve Mari. Her sister had kissed her gently on the forehead again and promised "I love you, ALWAYS, no matter what" before she laid Tina's head on the stiff bunk and allowed herself to be pulled out the door.

For the next ten days, Tina slipped in and out of consciousness but the guards never brought Mari back. On the eleventh day, when she was strong enough to walk, the guards drug her down a bright hallway, propping her up in front of an observation window at the end. She stared into the glass with horror, her knees buckling at the sight presented before her.

On the other side of the glass, Mari was strapped to an examination table wearing a simple paper gown that was drenched with sweat. Dozens of different fluids flowed into her from various tubes jammed brutally under her skin. Her eyes were rolled back into her head, chest heaving in distress. Tina tried to turn away but one of the officers held her head in place.

"*Look* at her! She did this for *you*! She tried to buy your freedom with her own life but she was a *fool*. You will swear your allegiance to Snow or you will die."

Releasing her head with a snap of his wrist, the officer and his companion began dragging her back down the hallway, away from the window, away from Mari.

"MARI! MARI!"

She had screamed her sister's name until her throat was raw and she had no fight left. Several more days passed but they gave her no insight into her sister's fate. By the time they opened her cell again, Tina had lost track of time. It didn't really matter. Mari was dead, she was sure of it, which meant she had nothing more to live for. No more reason to fight. She let them drag her down another hallway to a door that surprisingly led outside.

They dropped her on the ground in a heap, and she made no move to untangle herself. Footsteps came up behind but she made no effort to investigate. A fist gripped her hair and snatched her head back savagely to face the other person. She couldn't believe the face sneering back at her.

"*Mari*?" She had croaked as her head was released roughly. It couldn't be!

The woman staring down at her had her sister's face but her eyes were cold. Mari glared at her with no recognition, as if she didn't remember her own face, the face they shared. Dark circles under her eyes and cuts all over her body in various states of healing from where those tubes had been hastily removed, showed Tina how brutally her sister had been treated. An oversized tank hung off her gaunt body as she swayed unsteadily on her feet. When she pulled a revolver from her waistband, Tina didn't bother trying to defend herself. Mari was a mindless puppet and it was all her fault. Her sister had made a Faustian deal on her behalf.

"I'm so sorry Mari! This is all my fault. *Do it*! I forgive you." She whispered as she closed her eye,waiting for the shot.

It never came.

At that exact moment rebel forces had burst from the forest surrounding the compound. Snow's officers had grabbed Mari and pulled her back into the compound before she could be rescued. Troy and his team scooped Tina up and they disappeared into the tree line.

Months passed as Tina and her mother mourned their losses at the rebel base. It had broken her heart to tell their mother what had become of Mari and their father. She couldn't bear to look in the mirror; see her sister's face staring back at her. Even with the scars, the milky white eye that had once been hazel, it was still Mari's face that glared at her from inside the glass.

The first thing she did when she was strong enough was remove the massive curls that framed the face of a stranger. Gradually Tina came to terms with the loss of her eye as well. She began wearing a leather eye patch and answered primarily to Black Betty, her given name too painful to acknowledge.

In the absence of her father and sibling, she became the new face of the rebellion and took over leadership. The raids continued and the rebellion strengthened. Many came to believe that Black Betty was just a myth, a legend used by the rebels to disguise their true leaders. Some even thought that several different people filled the role.

The rumors worked in Tina's favor.

If Snow truly believed she was dead, he would be expecting no one to come for Mari. Every raid, Tina searched the officer's manifest in hopes of finding Mari.

The day they met again shook Tina to her core.

Chapter Four

Nearly a year had passed since the twins capture and Tina's escape.

Countless raids and information drops had yielded no hints as to Mari's whereabouts leading many to believe she was indeed dead. Troy had urged Tina to give up, to mourn her sister's loss and move on.

The two had grown close over the past few months: she, now the rebellion's commander and he her top lieutenant. She knew he meant well but she refused to turn her back on Mari, she could still *feel* her. Mari was out there, somewhere, and this time Tina would be the hero, save her. She owed her that much.

It had been a blazing hot day. Snow had gathered the people of the small township of Saint Andrew together in their makeshift town square for a rally celebrating his newly bought presidency. Tina, Troy and a few of their men were in the crowd waiting to see what Snow was up to this time. She had been leaning casually under a coconut tree with a baseball cap pulled down to disguise her face when the rally began.

A large, black Hummer pulled up near the stage and a dozen Snow Corp. soldiers moved through the crowd, forming a walkway from the vehicle to the stage. The door to the Hummer swung open, and Tina thought she would puke. The figure disembarked the vehicle in an immaculate white dress uniform, sword slung at their hip. A porcelain mask covered the upper part of the face but Tina knew those eyes. Knew those curls that her mother had cried for days when she had shaved hers off.

"Mari..." she gasped in a hoarse whisper, clinging to the tree for dear life.

Her sister moved through the crowd with the grace and poise she had always possessed, Tina being the brawler of the two. She moved to the platform and for just a moment, she locked eyes with her sister. Tina thought her knees would buckle at the notion that Mari would give them away. However, her sister simply smiled and nodded as she had done to several people behind Tina and continued to do until she reached the podium. Once there she stood ramrod straight, waiting for Bradford Snow to begin his speech.

"Is that? It can't be..."

Somehow Troy had made it to her side without her noticing. He grabbed her arm, trying to shake her out of her trance. Throughout the rally she stared at Mari but her sister never acknowledged her, never behaved like she had any idea who Tina was. As the affair was nearing its end, Tina had decided to simply grab Mari and run. She had been searching for over a year, she would not let Snow take her sister and disappear again. All her plans went to hell when Snow stopped speaking and gestured for Mari to approach the pedestal.

"Good people of Saint Andrew. I have come today to introduce myself. My name is Captain Mary Saint and I was once one of the rebels you glorify."

Murmurs spread through the crowd and Tina felt the urge to
puke quickly returning. Mary Saint? No wonder Mari hadn't
recognized her; she no longer even knew who *she* was. A cold
sense of dread began creeping through Tina's limbs. Even if
she grabbed Mari, her sister was obviously brainwashed,
unable to remember her former self. Taking her now could do
more harm than good. She was snapped back to attention as
Mari began to speak again.

"In my youth and inexperience, I thought that change was a
bad thing but President Snow took me in, helped me see the
error of my former ways. With great pleasure I offer my
services as Captain to the President's personal vessel *The
Magnus Q.* I, along with my men, hope to serve both the
president and you the people to the best of our ability. Thank
you."

Mari gave a short bow to the crowd and then a stiff salute to
President Snow, which he returned with a predatory smile.
That son of a bitch! He was dangling Mari in their faces but
keeping her just out of reach. His personal bodyguard?! They
would practically have to be on top of Snow to get anywhere
near Mari. He knew that anyone from the rebellion would
immediately recognize one of their fallen leaders. He was
trying to break their spirit by breaking Mari's mind. Tina and
her men had no choice but to watch Mari board Snow's
personal vessel and sail way.

The rally two nights before, when Mari was nearly killed, had
been eerily reminiscent of the first. The main exception had
been that Captain Saint, not Snow, was the main speaker.
Over the years, Mari had gained a fearsome reputation for
carrying out Snow's every sadistic order. She was feared by
all; spurring many in the rebellion to urge Tina to deal with
Mari, *permanently.* For her part, Tina never gave up hope that

she could free her sister. She and her mother had decided some time ago that if they could pry Mari from Snow, the three of them would disappear on *The Black Hammer* and rebuild their family. Suddenly that felt within their grasp.

Tina scaled the building once more; glad the heavy rains had dissipated for the night. Again she crept through the sliding glass door and to her sister's bedside. Mari had been propped up, a thin sheet pulled up to just below her ribcage, bandages exposed. Tina could see the scars she remembered all over Mari's arms and abdomen. Her mind flashed back to the image of tubes jammed brutally under her sister's skin and she shivered involuntarily.

She noticed Mari was shivering slightly too, so she grabbed the blanket from the end of the bed and covered Mari up to her neck. A sigh of contentment alerted Tina that her sister was waking up. She was relieved to see more color in her cheeks and the fact that Mari was mostly breathing on her own, save for the thin oxygen cord under her nose. Tina reached gently beneath the blanket to hold her hand.

"Hey," she rubbed her cheek gently with her free hand. " Mari, are you awake?"

Bleary hazel eyes met hers as Mari tried to shake off the effects of the drugs constantly being pumped into her and the exhaustion borne from a life-threatening injury. Not to mention it was 1:00 in the morning again. A small smile ghosted across her lips when Tina came into focus.

"You... came back?" She whispered hoarsely. Tina quickly grabbed a cup of water from the bedside table and held it to her sister's lips. Mari drank greedily before turning away.

"I told you I would." She reached forward to brush a few wayward curls out of her sister's face as Mari once again sighed in contentment. She leaned into Tina's warm touch and breathed as deeply as her injuries would allow.

"They said I was *crazy*. That..." she paused to gasp a little in pain. "... You didn't exist..." The statement put Tina on high alert.

"*Who* told you that?"

"Officer...a doctor..." Mari was fading again and who could blame her. Less than two days ago she had taken three bullets to the chest, the fact that she could even speak was remarkable in itself.

"Mari? Mari stick with me a little longer." Tina lightly slapped her sister's cheek trying to rouse her. Her sister cracked her eyes, trying to focus. "Honey, do you still have my gift?"

Mari nodded weakly before closing her eyes again and fumbled around for something on the other side of the bed. Tina grabbed her hand and placed it back under the blanket.

"Let me." She reached to the other side of the bed and was delighted when her fingers brushed something cool and round near Mari's thigh. "You hid it?"

"Ummm... couldn't let them know about... you." Mari's mind was fuzzy but she knew deep down that keeping this secret was important. Tina leaned forward and pressed her forehead to her sister's, trying to memorize the scent and feel of her.

"You were always the smart one." She quipped lightly. "I'll keep this safe for you, for *us*. We love you so much."

"*We*?" The word had piqued Mari's interest though her eyes remained closed. Tina nodded against her forehead.

"Yes, 'we'. Mami and I. The three of us are gonna be together again, I *promise*." There was a hard edge to Tina's voice as she realized the magnitude of her words but Mari needed hope. She needed a reason to fight the programming, to reclaim her life.

"Mami..." Mari repeated. "That would be...so...nice..." she whispered as she fell unconscious again. Tina leaned back and watched her sleep for a while before she moved across the room to Mari's charts hanging on the wall. She pulled out her phone, documenting all she could because if she was truly going to free her sister, she first needed to know what they'd been doing to her.

Once finished, she crossed back to the bed, making sure Mari was comfortable and warm. She tucked the blanket more securely around her, gazing at her sister's peaceful face. She tried to banish the image of that same beautiful face contorted in pain. No, this was how she should always be; at peace. Tina had to do anything she could to make that a reality for Mari.

She had no idea what horrors her sister had been facing in the time they'd been forced apart but she intended to find out, as soon as Mari was strong enough to hold a full conversation. Tina realized her visit was running long and reluctantly pressed one last kiss to Mari's temple before making her way out of the room and into the night.

Chapter Five

"You *can't* bring her back here."

Tina gaped in disbelief at that statement. She had just filled Troy in on her latest visit with Mari. How her sister was beginning to heal and more importantly, remember. How scared and confused Mari was and how desperately she wanted her life back.

Tina had taken everything she gathered from Mari's hospital records to the doctor's on her base. Her sister's life wasn't the only one ruined by Snow. Many other local youths had been taken forcefully over the years and their families could benefit too, if there was a way to break the programming.

Now, in her office away from prying eyes and listening ears, Tina revealed her budding plans to Troy; she was not prepared to be so soundly shot down.

"Are you kidding me?" Tina resisted the urge to yell, as the walls in their little base were not as thick as she would have liked. "Why can't I? This is where her family is. This is her **HOME**."

"No, it's not, not anymore. Mari isn't the same person that helped build this base and led this rebellion. It could be dangerous here for her..." Troy slumped against the wall, wrung out from trying to get Tina to understand. "She's in that hospital right now because someone on this base thought she had become too big a threat. Do you *really think* he's the only one?"

The thought actually had occurred to Tina, more than once. She had been horrified when one her own, one of the men she trusted with her life, broke rank and fired on her sister. The solider in question was currently being held in the brig, not for attacking Mari, but for ignoring orders.

How many more were there like him? People on this base who wanted her sister tried for her crimes or worse, dead? Could she really protect her? Mari couldn't be by her side all the time, not to mention, she would be unable to defend herself in her current state.

"This wasn't her fault! She *sacrificed herself* to protect me, this base and these people. She couldn't have known what they would make her… the things they would make her do!"

Troy moved from the wall and over to her. He reached a hand out, gently settling it on her upper arm. He tried to coax her into a hug, or at least into making eye contact with him. She did neither, instead staring numbly at the wall on the verge of tears.

"We've all suffered in this war." He reached up tracing her scars with the softest touch he could muster, resisting the urge to kiss her. Tina pulled away but only went a few steps before she whirled to face him.

"This!" She pointed emphatically at her patch before ripping it off to expose the wounds beneath. "This
is *NOTHING* compared to what they did to her. I lost my eye but Mari… she lost her whole identity, her *life*."

Troy stared at Tina in disbelief. He had only seen her without her patch a handful of times and they had been together for months before she had trusted him enough to let him see her scars. Now being faced with the damage again, he couldn't help but remember the last time she had been this open with him.

They had been lying in bed, quietly enjoying each other's company when he had gotten up to get a glass of water. When he returned, she had been sitting up in bed, idly flipping through a report, unaware she was being watched. Her patch lay on the nightstand and he was struck by how beautiful she was, even despite the scars.

"What?" She had inquired when she caught him staring, then in a moment of self-awareness, "My patch... I forgot..."

He had grabbed her hand before she could reach it. Assured her she didn't need it, didn't need to hide herself from him. Now, staring at those scars once again, he sought to reassure her.

"I didn't mean it like that." He pulled her into his arms despite her feeble attempts to escape him. She whimpered helplessly as he held her tightly against his chest before wrapping her arms around him in a fierce grip.

"It's all my fault." She whimpered again. "I *need* her! But I don't know how to help her. I don't know how to fix this."

Troy just nodded as he set his chin on top of her head and let her cry. The two stood entwined for several long, peaceful moments before Tina pulled away wiping her tears roughly. She bent to retrieve her patch before securing it into its usual position. She sniffed a little more then met his gaze.

"Thanks... I just needed to get that out I guess..." Troy nodded his understanding before asking a question that had plagued him for five years.

"What happened, Tina? To your face, to Mari? I remember she was there when we rescued you but we couldn't reach her."

Tina flopped ungracefully into her desk chair, motioning for Troy to sit in the chair across from her. For a long while she sat, fingers steeped, staring off into space before she cleared her throat and began to tell a story she hadn't been able to recount since it happened. She had often thought foolishly that not talking about it made it less real. Her nightmares had proven that to be a false hope, as her nights were peppered with heart-stopping moments of terror.

Even as she recounted the nightmarish chain of events that led to her disfigurement and Mari's assimilation, part of her couldn't believe that any of it had truly happened; that two people could endure such horrific events and still be whole in the end. Maybe that's why it hadn't felt real, because neither she nor Mari were truly whole, would ever be whole again. No, not until they were reunited... for good.

Throughout the entire retelling, Troy listened with a grim expression, afraid to interrupt Tina lest she become less forthcoming. When she stopped talking he had stared at her with both pity and a renewed sense of awe that she had held it together this long.

"That's ... that story was...um..."

"Horrific, nightmarish, bone-chilling, hard to believe that any survived?" Tina supplied in a flat voice.

"Yeah... all of that..." He whispered. Tina simply nodded in response, a faraway look in her eyes. "I'll help you."

"Help me what?"

"Save Mari. I'll help you save Mari." Tina's jaw nearly hit the floor at his announcement. "Now that I know what she's gone through and why, I can't just turn my back on her or you."

Tina continued to gape at him in disbelief, a single tear sliding down her cheek. He was going to help her; she wasn't alone. More importantly, Mari wasn't alone anymore. Someone besides Tina wanted to help her, help her take back her life and identity.

"Thank you..." she whispered as he rounded the desk and enveloped her in another crushing embrace.

"Don't thank me yet..." He responded ruefully.

"How are you feeling today, Captain?"

"Stronger than yesterday. A little bit better each day actually..." Mari had responded as the doctor carefully removed her bandages to check her wounds for infection. She hissed a little as he pressed on a particularly tender spot but he didn't seem worried.

"Good, good. All your wounds are healing quite nicely, remarkably in fact. I had no idea your 'enhancements' would be so efficient..." He clucked as he finished re-bandaging her chest, pulling the blanket back up to cover her.

"My what?" Mari was confused. She had heard the doctor telling an officer the same thing weeks before when she had first awoken. This was the first time in over a month at this hospital that anyone had mentioned it again. "What are you talking about?"

The doctor looked nervous as if he had said too much but then seemed to resign himself to her unnerving gaze. She had a right to know what was happening to her own body.

"Your 'enhancements'..." he began and Mari could almost see the air quotes. "Advanced gene engineering that allows you to be faster, stronger and heal more quickly. Apparently, every solider in Snow Corp. has them, though I always assumed it was just a rumor until you ended up in my O.R."

Mari nodded stiffly, digesting this interesting bit of information. She had a suspicion that the 'enhancements' did more than just make her a better solider, they had to have something to do with why she hadn't remembered Tina until just a few weeks ago. The doctor seemed to be watching her with a worried expression as if he had broken her somehow.

"How does it work?" She asked finally.

"I'm sorry..."

"The gene engineering, how does it work? Can it ever *stop* working?" The doctor seemed genuinely intrigued by her questions.

"Well, I'm no expert..." he began, pursing his lips in contemplation. "From what I can tell, the manufactured genes are unique to each host and when introduced to the body, they clasp onto the host cells and boost their production. The increase in cell production would, in essence, make you heal faster."

"I see. But could it stop working?" The doctor's expression went from thoughtful back to concerned. "Doc?"

"Yes… and no." Mari's expression pressed him to continue. "From what I can tell, the injections they've been having me give you reintroduce the manufactured genes into your blood. A booster shot of sorts."

"And without those?"

"Your regenerative qualities would be diminished. But continuing the treatments could have ill effects too. The engineered genes would never give up on their mission but, the human body can only take so much… eventually…"

"I'll burn out." Mari finished for him, her expression equally grim.

"Essentially." He agreed with her in a solemn tone. "It all depends on how long you've been on the therapy? How often you've been gravelly injured?"

Mari remained silent because the answers to both questions were less than promising. How long? Five years. How many injuries? Too many to keep track of. The enormity of his words hit her harder than the three slugs he had dug from her chest. She had been running full steam for so long, she couldn't possibly have much time left.

"If I stop right now, refuse more injections, what are my chances?" The doctor stared at her with a mixture of sympathy and caring. He took her hand in his own.

"My dear, I have no idea what you have been through but your scars tell a harrowing tale. At this point in your recovery, stopping the treatments may set you back substantially; perhaps even kill you. However, if you continue at the pace I suspect you have been going, you will 'burn out' as you put it, in just a few years. Is it worth it?"

"I don't know..." He patted her hand gently before setting it on the bed.

"You should rest. I will return tomorrow to check on you and bring your next injection. I'll leave you to decide how we proceed..."

He turned and crossed to the door, knocking twice to let the guard know to let him out. He gave her a small nod of reassurance as he stepped into the hallway, turning out her light as he went. Mari sat in the darkness, staring at the ceiling and wondering how she was going to break the news to Tina that she may not be worth saving after all.

Chapter Six

"Ugh!" Tina grunted with frustration as she slammed another Snow Corp. soldier's head against a wall.

She was irritated and tired, this raid being the fourth she had been on in a month looking for intel about Snow's brainwashing techniques. For weeks she had been visiting Mari, sneaking in, staying by her side for hours piecing together the years her sister seemed to have lost. She was secretly relieved every time Mari knew who she was because it seemed like only a matter of time before someone noticed and wiped that away for good.

Another solider emerged from a nearby hallway and she thought she would play with him a little. Why not? She could definitely use the outlet. He lunged at her with his sword, narrowly missing her midsection before his jaw connected heavily with her fist! He pulled back annoyed and readied himself to attack again.

Tina just smiled and beckoned him closer. He tried again, hefting a mighty swing that would have taken a less experienced fighters head off. Even with the use of one eye and the hood of her cloak up, Tina was a formidable fighter. As soon as she was well enough she had begun training with Troy to acclimate her fighting style to her disability. There were few swordsman with both eyes who could best her and this solider was nowhere near an expert.

Tina ducked easily, nicking the soldiers upper arm with her own blade to add insult *and* injury. Now the man was incensed, his attacks coming in a flurry of angry swipes! Tina dodged each one with practiced precision though a couple swings came dangerously close to connecting. She decided to stop playing with him and on his next charge, she used his momentum to duck under his arms and flip him over her back against the bulkhead! The impact made a satisfying clang that was music to her ears.

"Black Betty?" A familiar voice came through her earpiece.

"Yes, lieutenant? Find anything?"

"Yes ma'am, you're gonna want to see this!"

"Nice work. Pull everyone back to the Black Hammer."

"Acknowledged."

Tina's heart was racing as she made short work of a few more inexperienced soldiers' on her way back to the main deck. She had been expecting more of a challenge but suspected Snow kept his best fighters as close to him as possible. She made it to the deck and barreled towards the railing without hesitation before vaulting over it into darkness. Her feet collided with the deck of the Black Hammer mere seconds later. As soon as she landed she began giving orders.

"Disable cloaking, all sails at the ready, all hands on deck!"

The seamen on the scientific vessel in front of them were dumbfounded as the intimidating black vessel came into view. Its sails shimmered like oil, and the entire ship was made of dark smooth wood making it nearly invisible even without the cloaking device. The main mast flew a black flag with the usual skull and crossbones motif one would expect from a pirate ship. Just below flew a smaller flag depicting a sledgehammer with a golden crown hanging on it. The design had been their father's and both Tina and Mari bore that crown on their bodies. At the slightest movement, glittering cannon barrels automatically swiveled to put an end to the already disabled vessel.

"Ma'am? Cannons are at the ready. Waiting on your order to fire." A seaman informed Tina as he readied his finger over the launch button at the helm.

"At ease." Tina commanded.

"Ma'am?"

"Was I unclear seaman? I said *at ease*. The ship is incapacitated and they have no defenses. We got what we came here for. Set a course for the base. I'll be below decks. That is all."

"Aye, aye ma'am." The chastised seaman immediately went to work setting the necessary coordinates while avoiding Tina's scathing gaze as she headed to the lower decks. "All ahead full!"

Tina threw her hood back as she entered the stairwell; glad to be free of its stifling effects. It was a necessary evil, as it maintained an intimidating façade for Black Betty and disguised her identity but she never quite got used to it, no matter how often she wore it. Heading down a hallway she entered the first door on her right, the war room. Inside, a large metal table sat centered in a room surrounded by monitors of all sizes. Some showed security footage of the ship, others a live feed from the base, while others still showed various tapes obtained from their recent raids.

Troy stood before a large monitor, remote in hand watching and re-watching a tape they had just acquired. To his right stood the ship's medical officer, Rae Gomez, a pretty Mexican girl in her 20's that Tina was sure Troy had trysted with since their breakup. Tina did her best to still her jealousy as she approached the two, wondering what had captured their attention.

"You had something to show me Lieutenant?" She asked in a voice that clearly showcased her authority. As always in the field, Troy was all business.

"Yes ma'am. Dr. Gomez and I were just reviewing the tapes obtained in today's raid. Doctor?" Gomez looked slightly uneasy about having to address Tina directly. She cleared her throat and began speaking in a less than authoritative tone.

"Well... um, ma'am... These tapes seem to showcase some new techniques Snow hopes to use on his soldiers' in the near future. In the first few cases, it seems that they upped the doses of engineered genes given to the subjects. In the second set of tests, they tried combining the enhanced genes with cybernetic implants."

Tina listened carefully, trying to figure out why they insisted she hear this. She made a small motion with her hands encouraging the duo to keep talking.

"The results were... less than desirable..." Tina fixed the doctor with a hard glare.

"Clarify."

"In all cases ma'am, the subjects died within a few days of organ failure, stroke, heart attacks, brain aneurisms, you name it! From what I can tell, Snow and his mad scientists sacrificed at least 50 healthy young people. It was a huge loss so they decided to turn their trials on a
more *expendable* group." Gomez glanced at Troy for support and Tina instantly felt her anger rise until he spoke.

"They're going to start experimenting on those soldiers who are infirmed… or *injured*." He shot Tina a meaningful look and she felt as if all the air had left the room. Mari was a solider, an injured solider, in Snow's army. Tina groped blindly for a chair and sat with a defeated thud. Troy was instantly at her side. Gomez looked on confused.

"We have an… *informant* in Snow's army who was injured recently." Troy explained to the young woman. "It's their medical records you've been studying for the past few weeks. If this is true, they're in a lot of danger."

Gomez nodded numbly as her expertise was medicine, not extraction.

"Can we have the room please, doctor?" Somehow Tina had found her voice, just enough to dismiss the doctor.

Gomez seemed relieved to be excused and hurried back to the medical bay to further study the tapes. Once she was gone Troy sealed the door and took a seat across from her, waiting for her to say something.

"What do you wanna do?" He asked quietly.

"We're out of options. We have to bring her back to the base… the sooner, the better."

As soon as the ship docked, Tina stole away to the hospital. It was well past her normal visiting time yet Mari was awake when she arrived. It had surprised her to find her sister sitting up in bed, absentmindedly tracing the scars on her arm with her fingertips. She didn't even look up when Tina entered which put the other girl on high alert.

"Mari? Mari what's wrong?" Her sister still wouldn't meet her eyes.

"I have to tell you something… something that changes *everything.*" Tina sat on the side of the bed and gently tilted her sister's face up to meet hers.

"Sweetie what's going on? Just tell me."

"My enhancements," Mari began shakily barely able to hold Tina's gaze. " My enhancements… the side effects are… *fatal.* I only have a few years left at best… I'm so sorry I got your hopes up."

Tina went numb.

She had come here to warn Mari about the effects of what Snow was planning for her but it seemed he had already given her sister a death sentence. Tina drew her sister into her arms and did her best to comfort Mari as her shoulders shook in hushed sobs. Over the next few minutes she was able to coax a few more details out of her sister yet none of them made her feel any better.

If Mari quit now, she could be dead tomorrow and if she quit later, she could die suddenly of any of the terrible conditions Gomez had outlined earlier that day. Tina needed more time to figure this out, a luxury being denied them at every turn.

"Mari listen to me." She waited for her sister to look at her. "You have to keep taking the injections, just a few more days, until I can figure a way to get you out of here in one piece."

"Tina," Mari sighed as if she had already accepted her fate. "What good is that going to do?"

"Well for starters, the more injections you take, the stronger you'll be when I bust you out of here! And on the other hand, if you suddenly start refusing treatment, they'll be tipped off that something's different with you."

"And if I manage to escape? *Then what*? Instead of dying here, I die at the base where everyone around me wants me dead anyway?"

Tina stared at Mari in disbelief, dumbfounded that her sister had lost hope so quickly. Just the night before, the two had been discussing all the things they wanted see, traveling the world with their mother. Now Mari acted as if she already had one foot in the grave.

"Stop it! Stop acting like you're already dead. We've been given another chance and dammit we're gonna take it! I just need a little time." Tina grabbed her sister's shoulders and shook her more roughly than she intended, causing Mari to wince. Her expression softened when she noticed the pain etched across her sister's face. "I'm sorry! Did I hurt you? I just can't stand you talking about yourself like you're not worth it."

Mari nodded slowly, taking in her sister's words. Tina was so determined to help her but she worried doing so would in end in both their deaths. Still, if her sister believed they could do it, Mari would try. She couldn't disappoint Tina.

"Okay. I'll keep taking the injections, as long as you have a plan that doesn't put you in danger." Tina smiled broadly and waved a dismissive hand before hugging her sister much more gently.

"Danger is my middle name..." Mari made a face of disgust. "What?"

"Your middle name is 'Grace'." Tina rolled her eyes.

"Oh sure, *that* you can remember!"

She climbed into bed beside Mari and held her gently until Mari drifted into a slightly fitful but well-deserved slumber. Watching her sister sleeping soundly against her chest, Tina couldn't imagine getting Mari back only to lose her in a few short years. There had to be a way to reverse the effects or at the least extend her sister's life and she barely had 48 hours to find it. She had her work cut out for her. With a sigh she slid Mari off her chest onto the mountain of pillows required to keep her sister comfortable. Mari stirred but didn't wake, a testament to how truly exhausted she was from staying up all night contemplating her mortality.

"I'm not gonna let you die." Tina whispered to her sister as she tucked her in, placing a small kiss on her forehead. "I love you too much."

"Gomez!"

Tina burst into the medical bay on a mission for answers. The doctor nearly jumped ten feet in the air at her entrance, having been extremely focused on her laptop. She spun in her chair, clutching her chest staring at Tina wide-eyed.

"Commander! I mean ma'am! I mean… what are you doing here at this hour?"

Tina glanced at the clock. It was 4:30 in the morning, an hour no sane person ever saw on their bedside table. She couldn't care less about the time, she was on a strict clock and she could feel Mari slipping away from her with every second that passed.

"This is *my* base. I can be *anywhere* at *any* time I please." She gave Gomez her most intimidating stare before continuing. "I want a briefing on everything you've discovered about Snow's bioengineering."

"Of course… I'll have my staff pull it together…"

"Now."

"I'm sorry…"

"Brief me now. I don't have time for official reports." Tina pulled a rolling chair away from a table and sat facing the doctor, an expectant look on her face. Gomez swallowed hard and began.

"Well, it's pretty sophisticated…"

"I know it super-charges cell production and makes you heal faster. I also know that it has a major side effect in that it burns up your immune system. What I want to know is…can you slow the deterioration? Even stop it?"

The level of knowledge Tina had just displayed on the subject took Gomez aback. Tina knew the doctor must be suspicious as to how she became an expert in just a few hours but she didn't have time to play coy. Mari's demise was inching ever closer and this time around Tina intended to fight to keep her sister. She waited for the doctor to answer.

"From what my research indicates, the patient would have to be administered a high dose of the engineered cells and then slowly backed off the regimen with decreasing doses."

"Like a detox?"

"Essentially. However, there are a few hurdles to get over." Tina thought it sounded too easy.

"First of all, the patient would suffer painful withdrawal symptoms possibly even the re-opening of old wounds." Tina flinched at the thought of Mari bleeding deeply from the chest again. "Secondly, the treatment itself is difficult to duplicate and it has a shelf life of barely a day or so, which means we would be manufacturing the serum nearly round the clock, depending on how many patients we have."

The doctor sounded hopeful that she would be able to help more soldiers. It had long been Tina's plan to free those poor souls taken into Snow Corp. by force and that had been the carrot she had dangled in front of the doctor to garner her cooperation. Gomez had joined the resistance when her two younger brothers were taken and months later showed up in Snow uniforms. Tina didn't want to alienate her by saying that mission was no longer a priority so she lied.

"Your second concern shouldn't be a problem doctor. We'll only be trying this treatment on one patient to start, just to be sure its safe, so you should have no problem synthesizing enough serum."

"Your informant?" Tina nodded brusquely. The doctor didn't know Mari, she had joined the resistance barely a couple years ago; the fewer people who knew her sister's identity, the better. At least until Tina could guarantee her safety on the base.

"Yes..." Tina hedged. "I am concerned though that we don't have the medical resources to keep them comfortable during the detox period."

"Actually ma'am," Gomez stood and pulled back a curtain on the other side of the medical bay to reveal a dizzying array of medical machinery that Tina could only guess the uses for. "After we gathered the intel you wanted, I thought it might be beneficial for us to do a little 'shopping'? I was just finishing up the inventory when you came in." Tina couldn't hide how impressed she was.

"Nicely done, doctor. Nicely done." Tina moved forward to run a hand over one particularly shiny machine. "Now we just need a plan to get them out of that hospital and back down here safely."

"I think I might have an idea..."

Chapter Seven

Tina sat in the black van, restlessly drumming on the steering wheel as she kept a keen eye for potential threats. Glancing in the rearview mirror, she adjusted her Snow. Corp baseball cap making sure it cast a shadow over her injured eye. Her scars were far too conspicuous, one of the reasons she was stuck in the parking garage while Troy and Gomez were extracting her sister. She reached over nervously to the passenger seat, checking the charge on the device there. 100% the display read. Good. Now all she could do was wait.

"Are you ready?" Gomez asked the injured woman lying before her.

"For what? To die again? Not especially. But if your leader think this is the only way… Let's get this over with." Mari made sure not to refer to Tina by name as the doctor was unaware how deeply connected the two women truly were.

Gomez hesitated for just a second as she lifted the loaded needle to the woman's I.V. There was something so familiar about Mari yet she couldn't seem to place it. The woman's voice, her face, somehow she knew her.

"Doctor?"

She realized with a start that she had been staring and quickly shook her head to clear it giving the woman a thin smile before responding.

"Sorry. I don't usually do extractions... or, um , stop people's hearts.." Gomez whispered in a hurried explanation. Mari gave her a small smile in return.

"That's okay. Until recently, I didn't die this much."

Gomez gave a nervous laugh at the woman's attempt to set her at ease. Here she was about to stop this woman's heart and smuggle her out in a body bag yet her patient was trying to reassure her. Part of her was drawn to Mari, as if they had already met somehow, established a rapport. Gomez inserted the needle and met Mari's eyes.

"Deep breathes, okay? It's going to burn going in..." She told her with a grim expression. "Then when you wake up, hopefully you'll be far away from here."

Mari nodded before grabbing the doctor's arm, hastily. "Thank you. No matter what happens, thank you for try-..."

Mari gasped as a burning sensation spread up her arm and it into her chest before her world erupted in pain! She jerked off the bed, the movement pulling viciously at her newly healed skin as she choked and gasped.

Gomez watched the display, heard the monitors going wild before Mari fell limp on the bed. When the monitor announced Mari's flat line, the doctor jumped into action pretending to resuscitate her.

"What happened?!" The guard burst into the room, panic written large on his face.

"She flat-lined! Get help!" Gomez pointed him back towards the door just as Troy rushed in dressed as a nurse. "Get that tray and bring it here!" She ordered Troy.

He quickly brought the directed items to the bedside where Vasquez filled a large needle to the brim before plunging it into Mari's chest! To anyone else it would have appeared to be a shot of adrenaline to jumpstart Mari's heart, in reality it was a concoction designed to flush the other drug from the wounded woman's system so she could be resuscitated later. Troy glanced at his watch.

9 minutes left.

Their window to resuscitate Mari without permanent damage was rapidly closing. The lieutenant quickly raised the bars on Mari's bed and began pushing it out the door to an elevator; all the while Gomez sat atop Mari's chest administering CPR.

It wasn't just for show; she *had* to keep blood pumping to Mari's vital organs while she was in arrest. The guard came back around the corner as the doors to the elevator were closing.

"Operating Room 2!" Troy yelled to the harried guard, seemingly indicating their destination.

Once the doors closed, Gomez hopped down and began removing any and all medical devices from Mari before she helped Troy zip the woman up in a black coroner's bag, transferring her body to a waiting gurney.

4 minutes.

As soon as the doors reopened, Gomez exited and headed left while Troy pushed the gurney right, towards the morgue. Once inside he informed the medical examiner that the body was property of Snow Corp. and he had specific orders to deliver it to the van outside. He presented the annoyed old man with flawless forgeries of official transfer documents then wheeled the gurney out to the waiting black van.

When she saw Troy approach,Tina hopped out and helped him load the gurney, keeping her face neutral as if this were just another pickup. Sure the coast was clear, both she and Troy hopped back in and roared the van to life. Tina passed her lieutenant the baseball cap and jacket she wore before climbing in back to assist Gomez who had slid into the van unnoticed.

1 minute.

The pair unzipped the black bag as Tina handed the defibrillator to the young doctor. She locked eyes with Tina before rubbing the paddles together, holding them above Mari's chest.

"Here goes nothing..." She muttered. "Clear!"

The paddles slammed into Mari's chest before the current had her lurching off the gurney. She slumped back, still and unresponsive. Tina tried not to panic. Gomez adjusted a few knobs on the machine then prepared to go again.

"Clear!" She yelled again even though it was only the three of them in the van.

Troy tried to focus on keeping the van on the road but was shaken by the desperation in the doctor's voice. It *had* to have worked. Mari lurched upward again yet settled without signs of life.

No. They timed it. They did *everything* right.

"Again." Tina ground out, wild determination in her eyes. "Hit her again. *Please.*"

Gomez nodded before turning the machine up as high as it would go. If a charge this size didn't bring Mari back…

Without a second thought she slammed the paddles against Mari's chest! The injured woman arched so far off the gurney that Tina flinched when she came back down. The silence was thick in the van as they waited, and waited, and waited…

Tina broke down first.

"**NO**. Dammit, Mari! Wake up! You *have* to wake up!"

Tina slammed a fist against her sister's chest, then another. Over and over she pounded on Mari's chest as she cried tears of grief, of guilt, of the pure sorrow borne from the loss of her sibling, the other half of her heart. Troy stared at the road ahead in despair as he listened to Tina unravel. Gomez sat off to the side, glaring at her hands as if they had betrayed her.

How had she miscalculated?

Eventually, Tina ran out of steam and collapsed atop her sibling with a whimper, clinging to Mari's rapidly cooling body. The only sounds in the cramped cabin were sorrowful whimpers Tina emitted ever so often until ... a jagged moan escaped from their patients' lips as life poured back into Mari, followed by a string of painful coughs and stuttering breathes!

"Mari?" Tina shot upright and scrambled back in alarm! With disbelieving eyes, she reached out for her sister. Trembling fingers barely touched her injured sibling.

"Tina..." came the ragged response, though Mari's eyes remained squeezed shut in pain. A sharp cry tore through Tina as she fell upon her sister, kissing her tenderly.

"I'm here. I'm here, Mari. We're going home. *You're* going home." She told her sister as she wept quietly, her forehead pressed to Mari's in an effort to offer some form of comfort.

Troy nearly slumped over the steering wheel in relief when he heard the injured twin take that first breath. Gomez pulled her medical bag over and quickly began examining Mari to see if their stunt had caused any more damage to the woman's injuries. She gave Mari a shot for the pain surely caused by her CPR and resuscitation before checking the woman's wounds. All Mari's stitches had thankfully held and to everyone's relief, no one was pursuing them.

Tina met Gomez' eyes across the cabin and when the doctor gave her an affirmative nod, she lifted her sister's head into her arms, cradling her gently. She kept kissing the other girl, tenderly stroking her face. Mari was weak but managed to grip her sister's arm in response. Gomez watched the scene before her, overwhelmed that she had been able to save her commander's friend.

She watched quietly as Tina continued to cradle the other woman against her, unable to stop touching her, overcome with emotion. Indeed, to the doctor it seemed like the women were *more* than friends. In fact, from a certain angle, the two women looked quite similar. Like they could be related. Possibly siblings or...

"TWINS!" The doctor gasped startling everyone in the van. She pointed at Tina before shouting, "She's your twin!"

Tina said nothing, confirming the doctor's suspicions without a word. But something else nagged at the doctor. She'd never known Tina had a sister yet Mari had seemed eerily familiar. Gomez looked to Troy for answers.

"We couldn't tell you." Troy met her eyes in the rearview mirror. "There are a lot of people on the base who wouldn't be happy about Mari coming home."

"Why, because she's in Snow's army? Because she got hurt?" Gomez glanced at Mari once more, noting the location of her injuries, the timing, her height, build and affiliation with Snow. When it hit her, anger swelled inside Gomez like a firestorm. "Goddamit!"

Tina clutched her sister tighter, placing herself between Gomez and the gurney. She wasn't taking any chances as the doctor shook with rage.

"Please hear us out..." She beseeched, trying to keep her voice even.

"Hear you out?! Your sister is *Captain Saint*, the rebellion's worst enemy! She has done *terrible, horrible* things! And you tricked me into helping her!"

Gomez had never felt so betrayed in her life. She had felt a kinship to Mari, thought that perhaps she and the woman might have even been friends. But now, knowing who she was, what she represented... the very thought made the doctor sick.

"Doctor..." Mari rasped from her position against Tina's chest. "*Please*.... you don't... you don't understand..."

Mari was struggling to remain conscious enough to plead her case, yet the afternoon's events were rapidly sapping her of any strength she had left. Tina wrapped her arms more securely around her in an effort to comfort her sister despite the accusations being flung their way.

"It's okay. It's okay Mari, I'll tell her." Tina cooed as her sister drifted into unconsciousness. "I'll make her understand."

Mari nodded weakly before going still. Tina laid her back down gently on the gurney, turning to face the livid doctor. Vasquez stared her down, hate-filled eyes darting between the gurney and Tina unsure of whom she despised more."Well?" she demanded, arms crossed and posture rigid. "This better be good..."

Chapter Eight

Mari awoke to the sound of a distant beeping accompanied by an overall feeling of warmth and comfort. Turning her head to the side she gingerly opened her eyes; a figure slowly took shape before her. Recognition dawned immediately at the sight of tan skin, golden curls, and hazel eyes with just a hint of wrinkling at the corners.

"Mami?" She croaked, her throat dry from lack of use. It couldn't be? Could it?

At the sound of her voice, the figure slumped in a chair next to her bed bolted upright immediately! A warm hand squeezed hers tight as the familiar face drew closer, her mother hovering above her with tears in her eyes.

"Marisol? My baby! I knew you'd come back to us." A gentle hand cupped her face and Mari leaned happily into the warmth, inhaling the familiar scent of floral and coconut oil that lingered on her mother's skin.

"Where?" She asked, slightly confused as she struggled to sit up in bed.

The last thing she remembered was riding in a van with Tina, Troy, and the doctor feeling much worse than she currently did and deeply under suspicion. Another set of warm hands gently but firmly pushed her back into the soft bed. Her sister stood to her left, relief evident on her face.

"You're *home*, Mari." She explained simply. "And you need to rest." At the mere mention of the word, Mari felt her eyes getting heavy, fluttering closed briefly.

"Home?" she muttered, fighting her own drowsiness. "You kept your promise..." Her head tilted slightly toward her sister, wonder in her voice.

"You doubted me?" Tina hoped the hurt wasn't evident in her voice when she responded. Mari's next words assuaged all her fears.

"Never. Not for a moment..." she replied sleepily before her eyes slipped closed, a small content smile on her lips.

"Where is my captain?"

The question hung in the air, fraught with implications of guilt. Bradford Snow stood in his lavish office, the picture of wealth and opulence, a glass of aged scotch in hand as he awaited a response. He sipped quietly from the glass but never took his eyes off the view from his window as if he could spot Mari from here.

"According to all our intel, sir... she's... the Captain is *dead* sir."

Snow turned to face the man giving him this less than desirable report. The boy was barely nineteen, not a man at all; younger than his own son had been when he'd gone into battle. Snow's eyes narrowed as he spoke again.

"**Dead**? All previous reports had the Captain recovering remarkably well and now you tell me she's dead. Where, then, is *my* body? *She* belongs to me. You all do."

"We believe the rebels took it, sir. Though we have no idea why..."

Why? Snow smirked. Oh, he knew why. This had been a rescue mission. Somehow the rebels had figured out a way to liberate his favorite possession and he would not rest until she was returned.

"Find her."

"But, sir, she's de-"

"I said *find her*!

The man nearly tripped over his own feet trying to escape his leader's wrath. Snow waited for the boy to leave before crossing to his mantle and lifting a frame from it. There, taunting him behind the glass was Captain Saint. *His* Captain. He smirked at his reflection in the glass, at the pure ruthlessness of his taking August St. John's own child and turning her against his precious rebellion. An eye for an eye, a life for a life, a *child* for a child.

Yes, Mari was alive, on that he would bet his life. She would return to him, of her own accord he wagered because the rebels were not as innocent as they appeared. And Mari, for all the world a familiar face was also the beast that had carried out his every order. They would not easily take her back, if they would at all. And in that moment, when her desperation was high, she would flee back to the familiar arms of her master and help him *crush* the rebellion.

"Rest up my dear." He clucked as he set the frame down. "You and I still have much work to do."

When Mari awoke again, her sister was gone yet her mother remained at her side clutching her hand firmly. At the sound of her daughter's waking, Gaia quickly took a cup from the bedside table and offered it to the girl. Mari sipped from the straw gratefully before signaling she'd had enough.

"How are ya feeling baby? Would ya like some*ting* to eat?"

Mari smiled faintly as she listened to her mother's soft voice, tinged with island dialect. Neither she nor Tina had retained their island accent, their father's British accent overriding their speech, something she often regretted.

"It's just like I remembered," she mumbled happily. Her mother gently helped her shift into a sitting position, mindful of irritating her daughter's injuries. Mari's chest wounds were still healing, not to mention the cracked ribs she had suffered during her resuscitation the night before.

"What's dat?" Her mother inquired.

"Your voice, your accent." Mari told her with tears in her eyes. "I used to hear it in my dreams but I wasn't sure it was real. That *you* were real."

Throughout her captivity, Mari had dreamed of her mother, Tina and their family but she doubted its realism. After all, if she truly had a loving family, she wouldn't be *alone*; fighting in a war she didn't believe in. She had often wondered if she had made them up, imagined a family to make her solitude more tolerable. She was pulled from her musings when she realized her mother had enveloped her in a gentle, comforting embrace, her head cradled lovingly against her mother's bosom.

"Don't say dat! I'm real and ya gonna be alright. Mama's here!"

"I'm sorry..." she began, not sure what she was apologizing for. Her mother moved back and cupped her face in both hands, staring intently at her, willing her daughter to believe.

"Ya have *nothin'* to be sorry for. I dinnae care what anyone else says. You're home now and dis is where ya belong."

She waited for Mari to nod her understanding before she released her and began fussing over her once more, fluffing her pillows and tucking the blankets more securely around her. When Mari was sufficiently immobilized in a burrito of comfort, her mother climbed onto the bed with her, pulling her to her chest again. Mari sat back and enjoyed the attention, the gentle hands soothing her aches, stroking her hair. As she melted deeper into her mother's embrace she thought that maybe Tina had been right; maybe it would all be okay in the end.

There was an audible slap as Tina closed the file on her desk and shoved it aside. She pinched her brow between her thumb and forefinger trying to ward off an oncoming headache from poring over supply reports and mission briefings. She'd been at it for several hours, finding it hard to concentrate knowing her sister was just a short walk away. Mari was doing well, responding to the treatment and stronger than she was less than a day before yet Tina still felt uneasy. When the phone rang on her desk, she knew why...

"Commander?!" Gomez panicked voice crackled through the receiver, putting Tina instantly on alert.

"Doctor? What's wrong? It's Mari, isn't it?" Tina could feel her chest tighten as she awaited a response.

"You need to come to the med-bay, ma'am! Right **now**."

Tina slammed the phone down and barreled out the door. She stormed through the halls, ignoring concerned looks until she reached the med-bay. Pausing outside the doors, she took a moment to compose herself before stepping inside to be immediately swallowed by the chaos.

"Commander!"

Gomez spotted her near the door and charged over, expertly navigating equipment and personnel. Grabbing Tina's hand, she pulled her into the small private room Mari had been resting in since her arrival, protecting her from prying eyes.

"Doctor, **what** is going on?" The doctor gestured towards the center of the room before answering her question.

Medical personnel poking, prodding and monitoring her condition surrounded Mari's bed. She looked worse than Tina had seen her in weeks. Her face was pale and drawn, dark circles forming under each eye. Her chest rose and fell raggedly, aided by a ventilator. There was no trace of the vibrant woman her sister knew and loved.

"She's *crashing*. The serum we synthesized just isn't strong enough." Gomez had a grim expression as she explained the dire nature of the situation.

Tina eyed Gomez warily. The doctor had reacted poorly to the news of who Mari truly was and had initially refused to treat her. One look at the other woman's face confirmed what Tina already knew. The doctor had sworn an oath to do no harm and would keep to it no matter how she felt about the patient personally. Before she could inquire further or process the doctor's words, her mother appeared.

"Bettina!" Gaia rushed up to her upset and shaking. Tina hugged her mother instinctively, trying to comfort her.

"Mami, what happened?"

"I don't know! She was fine, sitting up and eatin' on her own. Then she started coughing, said she couldn't breath. By the time the doctor got here, she had collapsed!"

"It's okay Mami. It's gonna be okay." She turned determinedly to Gomez. "What can we do doctor? We've come too far, I won't lose her now."

"I don't know why our serum isn't working but her old doctor might. If he could help us with the formula, she might have a chance…"

"How long does she have?"

"Twelve hours; maybe a day…" Gomez couldn't hide her hopelessness. Despite everything else, she had hoped Mari would live, if only for her family's sake. "We need that doctor **NOW**."

Tina nodded stiffly then turned back to her mother. "Mami, stay here with her. Help the doctor and keep her comfortable. I'll be back as soon as I can."

She grabbed her watch and set the timer feeling more panicked by the second as it counted back from 12 hours. She left the room, pausing to use the doctor's phone.

"Lieutenant!" she barked into the receiver. "I need you and two of your best men. Discretion is key. Wheels up in 15."

"Yes ma'am!"

Tina quickly left the med-bay and headed for her quarters. There were several items she would need to make this mission a success and it *had* to succeed. She barely made it in the door before the sobs wracked her body. Sliding down the wall she felt the despair wash over her. Why? Why Mari? Why now? It seemed that no matter how hard Tina tried, there was always another obstacle in her way. The sounds of her misery filled the small space for several minutes before she managed to compose herself.

"Get it together Tina..." she mumbled angrily, wiping roughly at her face.

Picking herself up off the floor, she quickly gathered her supplies. Sparing a glance in the mirror on the way out she noticed her nose was red, cheeks flushed and her eye was bloodshot. She assumed the situation beneath her patch was even worse but there was no time for vanity. Mari trusted her when she had said it would all be okay, she had to make good on that promise.

Chapter Nine

It will be OK. I will make it OK.

Tina chastised herself harshly as she advanced toward the harbor, her overflow sack blasting at the creases with hardware, threw over her lean shoulders. She slouched under its heaviness, yet she wouldn't try to ease her burden in case she leave something she really required; something imperative to her central goal. With the hood on her shroud set up, she needed to tip her head back to see the Lieutenant close to the edge of the dock. Troy met her with a concerned articulation.

"Officer, we're prepared to push off ma'am." Troy illuminated her; the way where he focused on "we" struck her as odd.

"What's up, Lieutenant?"

Troy glared and snatched her elbow, directing her away from the men in case they catch wind of.

"The gathering needs to address you. About Mari." He murmured faintly.

"They'll simply need to stand by. We've burned through enough time as of now." She turned on her heel to load up the vessel however he pulled her back generally!

"No, Tina. They need to address you, NOW."

Tina scowled at him, totally insulted by the harsh taking care of and the way that he had tested her before their subordinates. He appeared to acknowledge how he had treated he immediately dropped his hand.

"See, I'm unfortunately assuming you go with us...They may settle on a choice while you're gone above and beyond won't like."

"What are you talking about, Troy?" Panic streaked through Tina at the possibility of another person settling on choices about her sister's prosperity.

"I simply think you would be wise to remain. Converse with them... ensure Mari. I swear I'll track down that specialist for you. I will not bomb you, or her."

He was correct; Tina realized that. Mari's return was a political bad dream. Almost certainly there would be requests for equity, revenge... what's more discipline. Assuming that Mari endured the evening, what sort of life could she confront? Shoulders drooped in shame, she passed Troy her pack.

"You need to track down that specialist." She begged him.

"I will. I told you, I will not fizzle." He pressed her arm reassuringly prior to delivering her. Amazingly, Tina inclined in and pecked him softly on the cheek.

"Much thanks to you." She murmured prior to turning, squaring her shoulders and heading back up the dock to stand up to the committee.

"Administrator, so great of ye ta go along with us." A reed-slight man with a profound Caribbean complement, chocolate skin, and a tuft of subsiding white hair tended to her with not at all subtle scorn.

"I was taken off on a touchy mission when you called me." A reality handily confirmed as Tina presently wore her mark hooded shroud, blade next to her. "I really do trust this is significant, Lord Blackman."

The elderly person was not genuinely a "ruler", not in the conventional sense. Each individual from the board had been an innovator by their own doing, most from little municipalities that Snow and his men had overwhelmed. Despite the fact that Tina was the primary individual seeing to the everyday business of the insubordination, her dad had framed the board to keep working assuming the nonentity should fall. Typically, they paused for a minute and permitted Tina to settle on the difficult decisions and she had rapidly realized, when they reached out, horrible would happen to it.

"Gracious it is. It's absolutely critical to you, Commander." The elderly person warbled accordingly. "For this matter worries your sister, Marisol."

Tina solidified at the affirmation that the committee realized Mari was back and were obviously despondent with regards to it.

"Shouldn't something be said about Marisol?" She asked equally.

"Is it genuine she is alive?"

"Indeed."

"Is it genuine she is presently on dis base?"

"Indeed."

"What's more is it likewise evident, Commander, dat de very individual ye are tryna secure is additionally our most prominent foe?!"

The elderly person brought his voice up in allegation and pointed a shriveled finger at Tina. There were stunned and disliking mumbles all through the room however Tina would not be occupied, maintained eye contact with the elderly person savagely.

"Marisol isn't Saint. Not any longer." Tina attempted frantically to keep her voice even.

"Furthermore we're guessed ta believe you?"

"What's truly going on with this gathering?" Tina countered.

"For's about equity." Tina recoiled at the accentuation the elderly person set on the word. "Your sister has perpetrated unspeakable wrongdoings, numerous against de individuals of dis base."

"She was influenced quite a bit by. You can't consider her answerable for that!"

"Lair who do we consider capable?"

"Marisol helped lead this defiance! She forfeited herself for myself and for every one of you! She never needed to battle. I persuaded her it was the proper thing to do. What's more I have been driving this insubordination since the time I lost her."

"Are ye saying we have ta follow you truly? Dat your choices are ta go unchallenged?" "When I make supply runs, do you doubt me? When I battle, disfigure and kill for the sake of this resistance, do you doubt me?"

Dis isn't something similar "

"Goodness, yet it is! I give EVERYTHING to this reason. In any case, you won't take this from me. You won't take her from me."

Tina hammered her hands on the table and stood, frowning at every individual from the gathering trying them to challenge her once more.

"Marisol won't be being investigated in your court or some other. She is under my insurance and any individual who needs to challenge me on that is free to do as such. I'll be waiting...sword close by."

"You would undermine your own kin?!"

"You are not my kin! Not anymore..." Tina pummeled her hands on the table again prior to adding. "Perhaps it's time this base found a new leader..."

It was an unfilled danger. She knew none of the gathering individuals really needed to lead. They professed to have individuals' inclinations on a fundamental level however not a solitary one of them were able to take care of business. Assuming they thought she was thinking about venturing down, perhaps it would be the influence she expected to secure her sister.

"Leader, dere's no need ta be impulsive!"

Tina grinned deep down. There it was. Concession. She lifted her eyes to meet the elderly person's.

"Nobody outside this room is to realize Marisol is back. On the off chance that I even hear a murmur regarding my sister, anyplace on this base, I won't spare a moment to leave it and you without a leader. And afterward you can sort out who needs to play 'Dark Betty' next."

Tina stepped unquestionably to the entryway before she stopped and looked behind her. "Assuming you want me, I'll be in the hospital."

Seven hours left.

Tina had lifted her arm for the 100th time, to look at her wrist. She ought to have gone as well; they required her on this mission. In any case, Troy had been determined that she stay, support her mom and solace Mari assuming she stirred.

Also her not-really lovely gathering with the board.

Some portion of her realized it was all in all correct to remain. The other half was climbing the dividers fully expecting accomplishing something, anything helpful. It was the center of the evening. Gomez had resigned to a bed in her office, her mom was nestled into the emergency clinic bed close to Mari's while Tina sat drooped in a firm upheld seat pausing and wishing. She propelled herself up, staggering to her sister's bedside.

"Hello." She murmured to the inclined structure, a shell of her sister with scarcely any life left. She laid a hand on Mari's brow and the other held her sister's furiously. "You want to hold tight somewhat longer. That specialist will be here any moment and he will assist you with simply enjoying he did previously. I didn't bring you here to pass on... so... so quit appearing as though you're not kidding."

She gazed at her sister with tears obscuring her vision yet there was no reaction. The main sound in the room was the engineered mood of the ventilator as it ensured Mari's chest proceeded to rise and fall. Tina inclined in nearer, brow squeezed against her sisters.

"Do you recall when we were nine? I got the chicken pox and Mami said that you needed to avoid our room so you wouldn't become ill as well. What's more ordinary you would sit just external the room and talk with me and shading, watch films, anything I desired to do. Furthermore consistently after Mami headed to sleep you would sneak in and nestle with me."

Tina snickered a little at the memory, reviewing that at the time her mom couldn't sort out how Mari had become ill too when the two young ladies had been isolated. She sat back a bit so she could gaze at her sister's dozing structure, brushing rebellious twists from her face.

"At the point when you became ill, it didn't make any difference to me that I felt better since you were languishing. So I did all that you had accomplished for myself and you improved two times as quick! Do you recollect what the specialist said? He said 'twins generally think about their kin first since one isn't entire without the other'. He was correct. I'm not entire without you so kindly, if it's not too much trouble, remain with me this time. Alright?"

"Bettina?" a languid sound came from her left. Tina cleaned her face generally prior to turning towards the sound.

"Mami, I'm heartbroken. Did I wake you?" Gaia sat up and tossed the sweeping back moving toward her girl.

"S'okay child. I'll keep watch, you rest now." She enveloped Tina by a warm, nurturing embrace.

"I can't rest ... " she muttered against her mom's chest. Before Gaia could demand there was a rattle from the workplaces right external the room. Tina hardened prior to pushing her mom behind her. "Remain with her Mami." She murmured through held teeth as she drew her sidearm.

Her mom knew not to contend, so she moved rapidly and unobtrusively to not entirely set in stone to secure her. Tina pushed the entryway open scarcely a break, worming through the little opening. The clinic was dull and calm; the main sounds a periodic blare from clinical hardware checking the patients. Toward her right sat the specialist's office, the light actually off showing she hadn't awoken from the sound. An aggravation to one side made them duck with perfect timing to stay away from a firmly grasped clench hand!

"We would rather not hurt you." A gravelly voice illuminated her as she obstructed another blow and encountered a covered aggressor. "We just need her."

"Who are you?!" She requested, weapon evened out at the veiled man.

"Concerned residents."

We? Residents? Tina felt her heart grasp at the majority of the words. There was more than one of them she understood as she spun on schedule to fire on a figure clad in dark attempting to slip into Mari's room! She could hear her mom howl from inside the room as the shot associated, the debilitated sound of lead punching through tissue. The man tumbled to the floor and Tina went somewhat to see the pool spreading consistently underneath him.

"Hell!" The main man cried. "You couldn't simply allow us to
have her!" He accused Tina of a carnal power that brought
down her over a close by work area as he hustled out the
entryway.

"What the heck?!" Gomez was remaining in her entryway,
face white at the scene before her.

"Watch him!" Tina hollered as she barreled out the entryway
after the principal man.

She arrived at the foyer and froze uncertain of what direction
to head before she heard unglued strides in the corridor
simply ahead. Tina dashed around the bend to capture them
when her reality went blindingly white!

Something had hit her from behind with enough power to
make her debilitated to her stomach. She staggered a couple
of more feet, sidearm dropping en route, before she imploded
to the virus floor.

There didn't be anything she could do as a couple of solid
hands got her wrists and started hauling her away.

"MARI!"

Gomez staggered out the diagnostic room in a frenzy, having quite recently wrapped fixing up the man Tina had quelled. Her blood ran cold at the shout that reverberated all through her prescription narrows. She pushed the way to Mari's room open and froze. The twins mother remained by the unfilled bed, mouth agape, eyes wide with awfulness.Mari was gone, leaving behind a few ridiculous spots and a disposed of breathing cylinder. Had she eliminated it herself? How on earth had Snow's crazy lab rats treated her that could permit somebody to accomplish something so frightful?"Where could she be? She couldn't simply leave, right?"Gaia was upset and understandably. Her lethargic little girl had ascended from her deathbed, eliminated her breathing cylinder and vanished."Tina! We really want to track down Tina."Gomez froze. Tina. Gracious, no. No, she was unable to have. The specialist turned to confront Gaia."I think I know where she went..."

www.ingramcontent.com/pod-product-compliance
Lightning Source LLC
Chambersburg PA
CBHW072120150726
47999CB00005B/2044